EMMA'S STORY

DEBORAH HODGE

Illustrated by

SONG NAN ZHANG

Tundra Books

Published in Canada by Tundra Books,
481 University Avenue, Toronto, Ontario M5G 2E9

Published in the United States by Tundra Books of Northern New York,
P.O. Box 1030, Plattsburgh, New York 12901

Library of Congress Control Number: 2003103801

National Library of Canada Cataloguing in Publication

Hodge, Deborah
        Emma's story / Deborah Hodge ; illustrated by Song Nan Zhang.

ISBN 0-88776-632-3

        I. Zhang, Song Nan, 1942- II. Title.

PS8565.O295E44 2003   jC813'.6   C2003-901706-0

We acknowledge the financial support of the Government of Canada through the
Book Publishing Industry Development Program and that of the Government of
Ontario through the Ontario Media Development Corporation's Ontario Book
Initiative. We further acknowledge the support of the Canada Council for the Arts
and the Ontario Arts Council for our publishing program.

Design: Kong Njo
Printed and bound in Hong Kong, China
1 2 3 4 5 6   08 07 06 05 04 03

For Katie Mia Wei Qiong, with love.

AUTHOR'S NOTE

All of us want to know our stories. For children, the story of their place in the family and how they came to be there is especially important.

A child grows and flourishes in the care of a loving family. Today's families can be biologically linked or they can be created through love and choice, as in the case of adoption.

When a child from one country is adopted by parents in another, it serves as a remarkable reminder that the world is a single community – where the joys and responsibilities of caring for children are shared by us all. Families created through international adoption form a bond of love that transcends distance and boundaries and builds cultural ties from east to west and north to south.

Every child, in every country, deserves and needs loving parents. International adoptions provide a way for children around the globe to have that opportunity.

ACKNOWLEDGEMENTS

With warm thanks to my dear friend, Eileen Power, for sharing her stories with me, especially the story of meeting her daughter, Katie, in China. A special thank you to Kathy Lowinger and Tundra Books for publishing my first picture book, and to Song Nan Zhang for creating such lovely paintings. I am grateful to you all.

Emma and Sam were making cookies at Grandma's house. Marley sat by the table, gobbling up bits of dough as they fell.

"Let's make a cookie family, Sam," said Emma. She used the middle-sized cookie cutter to make Sam. She used the big one to make Mommy and Daddy, and a dog-shaped one for Marley.

Sam used the big cookie cutter to make Grandma and Grandpa and the smallest one to make Emma. Emma and Sam each decorated their cookies.

"Buttons. Yummy!" Emma giggled as she pressed candies into the dough.

When Grandma took the cookies out of the oven, she said, "What a lovely family you've made."

"It's *our* family, Grandma. There's Mommy and Daddy, and you and Grandpa, and Sam and Marley and me. But look! I'm the only one with black hair and dark eyes." Sam had used raisins and strings of licorice to decorate the Emma cookie. Big tears rolled down Emma's cheeks. "I want to look like everyone else," she said.

Grandma gave Emma a warm hug. "Would you like to hear your story again?" Emma nodded.

Grandma sat down in her old stuffed chair and Emma climbed into her lap. She held Panda tight.

"Once upon a time, there was a Mommy and a Daddy who had a boy named Sam," said Grandma.

"And a dog called Marley," said Emma.

"They were a very happy family, except for one thing – they wanted a baby girl. Mommy said, 'If I had a baby girl, I'd wrap her in a soft quilt and sing her sweet lullabies.' Daddy said, 'If I had a daughter, I'd show her the ducks in the pond and push her on the swings.' Sam said, 'If I had a sister, I'd give her my toys and teach her all the games I know.' Marley thought, *If I had a little friend, I'd take her for walks and show her the neighborhood.*

"The family waited and hoped, hoped and waited, but a baby girl did not come . . . until one day Mommy and Daddy heard about a baby girl in China who needed a family. Her name was Li Ming. It meant bright and beautiful. Her hair was soft and black. Her eyes were deep dark brown. The baby was coming to live with them! They would call her Emma Li Ming."

"**E**veryone helped to get ready for Emma. Mommy set up a crib and painted lovely designs on the bedroom walls. Grandma sewed a soft quilt. Grandpa built a wooden toy box, and Sam filled it with toys. Daddy bought a stroller. Marley held his leash in his mouth and wagged his tail.

"Mommy and Daddy took a long plane trip across the ocean, to the other side of the world. They were going to bring Emma to her new home. When they got to China, Mommy and Daddy went straight to the big building where Emma lived with other babies and the aunties who cared for them."

"An auntie walked up to Mommy and Daddy carrying Emma in her arms. She smiled. 'Here is your new daughter.'

"Mommy held the baby close. With glistening eyes, she said, 'Emma Li Ming, I am so happy to meet you.' Daddy stroked Emma's soft hair and said, 'Hello Emma. We are your new parents. We will love you always.' Emma smiled shyly at Daddy and nestled deeper into Mommy's arms."

"That first night, Mommy, Daddy, and Emma stayed in a hotel. Mommy and Daddy cuddled Emma. They fed her and changed her and bathed her. They played peekaboo and Emma laughed. They marveled at her toes and fingers, and gazed into her deep, dark eyes.

"When Emma got tired, Mommy wrapped her in the quilt that Grandma had made and sang sweet lullabies until the baby fell asleep.

"The next day, Mommy and Daddy carried Emma proudly in their arms. They went to the park and to shops and to markets. Emma laughed and pointed at the birds, the trees, and the people on bikes and motorcycles. She delighted in the colors and sounds of the city. Mommy and Daddy delighted in Emma.

"A merchant gave Emma a toy – a furry black and white panda. 'It is a gift from China,' he said."

"Mommy and Daddy took Emma home on the plane. It was a long trip, but none of them noticed. Emma held Panda in her arms. Mommy and Daddy held Emma in their arms."

"At the airport, Grandma, Grandpa, Sam, and all the aunts, uncles and cousins were waiting to meet Emma. Marley was waiting in the car.

"Sam held up a big sign he'd painted. WELCOME HOME EMMA, it read.

"Everyone cheered and clapped when they saw Emma and Mommy and Daddy. Some people had joyful tears in their eyes."

"The next day, the whole family came to Grandma and Grandpa's house and had a welcome home party for Emma. Everyone brought food and presents for the new baby.

"Grandma and Grandpa kissed Emma. The aunts and uncles and cousins all took turns holding her. 'Welcome to our family,' they said.

"Sam played patty-cake with Emma, and Marley gave her a welcome-home lick."

"And from that day on, Emma and her family lived happily ever after," finished Grandma.

Just then, Mommy and Daddy came through the door. Emma ran to give her parents a hug. "I made you some cookies," she said. "Come see."

Grandma called Grandpa and Sam, and the whole family ate cookies with milk and tea. Emma snuck a big piece of cookie to Marley. He thumped his tail on the floor.

"That was a good story, Grandma," said Emma.

"You must have heard it a million times!" said Sam. Everyone laughed, including Emma.

"It's not how we look that makes us a family, Emma. It's how we love each other," said Grandma.

"And we love each other a *lot*!" said Emma.

When the family walked to the park, Emma held Marley's leash. She helped her daddy feed the ducks in the pond. Then Daddy pushed Emma on the swings while Sam called to her to pump her legs.

"Higher, Daddy, higher." Emma laughed.

Mommy snapped a photograph.

In a few years, when Emma is older, Mommy and Daddy will take her to China to show her the country where she was born. For now, Emma is happy playing in the park with her family.